THE HYENA

BY

ROBERT E. HOWARD

British Library Cataloguing-in-Publication Data
A catalogue record for this book is available from the
British Library

Robert E. Howard

Robert Ervin Howard was born in Peaster, Texas in 1906. During his youth, his family moved between a variety of Texan boomtowns, and Howard – a bookish and somewhat introverted child – was steeped in the violent myths and legends of the Old South. Although he loved reading and learning, Howard developed a distinctly Texan, hardboiled outlook on the world. He became a passionate fan of boxing, taking it up at an amateur level, and from the age of nine began to write adventure tales of semi-historical bloodshed. In 1919, when Howard was thirteen, his family moved to the Central Texas hamlet of Cross Plains, where he would stay for the rest of his life.

At fifteen Howard began to read the pulp magazines of the day, and to write more seriously. The December 1922 issue of his high school newspaper featured two of his stories, 'Golden Hope Christmas' and 'West is West'. In 1924 he sold his first piece – a short caveman tale titled 'Spear and Fang' – for $16 to the not-yet-famous *Weird Tales* magazine. He published with the magazine regularly over the next few years. 1929 was a breakout year for Howard, in that the 23-year-old writer began to sell to other magazines, such as *Ghost Stories* and *Argosy*, both of whom had previously sent him hundreds of rejection slips. In 1930, he began a

1

correspondence with weird fiction master H. P. Lovecraft which ran up to his death six years later, and is regarded as one of the great correspondence cycles in all of fantasy literature.

It was partly due to Lovecraft's encouragement that Howard created his most famous character, Conan the Cimmerian. Conan – a barbarian-turned-King during the Hyborian Age, a mythical period of some 12,000 years ago – featured in seventeen *Weird Tales* stories between 1933 and 1936, and is now regarded as having spawned the 'sword and sorcery' genre, making Howard's influence on fantasy literature comparable to that of J. R. R. Tolkien's. The Conan stories have since been adapted many times, most famously in the series of films starring Arnold Schwarzenegger.

Howard was enjoying an all-time high in sales by the beginning of 1936, but he was also deeply upset by the ill health of his mother, who had fallen into a coma. On the morning of June 11, 1936, he asked an attending nurse whether she would ever recover, and the nurse replied negatively. Howard walked to his car, parked outside the family home in Cross Plains, and shot himself. He died eight hours later, aged just thirty.

From the time when I first saw Senecoza, the fetish-man, I distrusted him, and from vague distrust the idea eventually grew into hatred.

I was but newly come to the East Coast, new to African ways, somewhat inclined to follow my impulses, and possessed of a large amount of curiosity.

Because I came from Virginia, race instinct and prejudice were strong in me, and doubtless the feeling of inferiority which Senecoza constantly inspired in me had a great deal to do with my antipathy for him.

He was surprisingly tall, and leanly built. Six inches above six feet he stood, and so muscular was his spare frame that he weighed a good two hundred pounds. His weight seemed incredible when one looked at his lanky build, but he was all muscle--a lean, black giant. His features were not pure Negro. They more resembled Berber than Bantu, with the high, bulging forehead, thin nose and thin, straight lips. But his hair was as kinky as a Bushman's and his color was blacker even than the Masai. In fact, his glossy hide had a different hue from those of the native tribesmen, and I believe that he was of a different tribe.

It was seldom that we of the ranch saw him. Then without warning he would be among us, or we would see him striding through the shoulder-high grass of the veldt, sometimes alone, sometimes followed at a respectful distance by several of the wilder Masai, who bunched up at a distance from the buildings, grasping their spears nervously and eyeing everyone suspiciously. He would make his greetings with a courtly grace; his manner was deferentially courteous, but somehow it "rubbed me the wrong way," so to speak. I always had a vague feeling that the black was mocking us. He would stand before us, a naked bronze giant; make trade for a few simple articles, such as a copper kettle, beads or a trade musket; repeat words of some chief, and take his departure.

I did not like him. And being young and impetuous, I spoke my opinion to Ludtvik Strolvaus, a very distant relative, tenth cousin or suchlike, on whose trading-post ranch I was staying.

But Ludtvik chuckled in his blond beard and said that the fetish-man was all right.

"A power he is among the natives, true. They all fear him. But a friend he is to the whites. *Ja.*"

Ludtvik was long a resident on the East Coast; he knew natives and he knew the fat Australian cattle he raised, but he had little imagination.

The ranch buildings were in the midst of a stockade, on a kind of slope, overlooking countless miles on miles of the finest grazing land in Africa. The stockade was large, well suited for defense. Most of the thousand cattle could be driven inside in case of an uprising of the Masai. Ludtvik was inordinately proud of his cattle.

"One thousand now," he would tell me, his round face beaming, "one thousand now. But later, ah! Ten thousand and another ten thousand. This is a good beginning, but only a beginning. *Ja.*"

I must confess that I got little thrill out of the cattle. Natives herded and corralled them; all Ludtvik and I had to do was to ride about and give orders. That was the work he liked best, and I left it mostly to him.

My chief sport was in riding away across the veldt, alone or attended by a gun-bearer, with a rifle. Not that I ever bagged much game. In the first place I was an execrable marksman; I could hardly have hit an elephant at close range. In the second place, it seemed to me a shame to shoot so many things. A bush-antelope would bound up in front of me and race away, and I would sit watching him, admiring the slim, lithe figure, thrilled with the graceful beauty of the creature, my rifle lying idle across my saddle horn.

The native boy who served as my gun-bearer began to suspect that I was deliberately refraining from shooting, and he began in a covert way to throw sneering hints about my womanishness. I was young and valued even the opinion of a native; which is very foolish. His remarks stung my pride, and one day I hauled him off his horse and pounded him until he yelled for mercy. Thereafter my doings were not questioned.

But still I felt inferior when in the presence of the fetish-man. I could not get the other natives to talk about him. All I could get out of them was a scared rolling of the eyeballs, gesticulation indicative of fear, and vague information that the fetish-man dwelt among the tribes some distance in the interior. General opinion seemed to be that Senecoza was a good man to let alone.

One incident made the mystery about the fetish-man take on, it seemed, a rather sinister form.

In the mysterious way that news travels in Africa, and which white men so seldom hear of, we learned that Senecoza and a minor chief had had a falling out of some kind. It was vague and seemed to have no especial basis of fact. But shortly afterward that chief was found half-devoured by hyenas. That, in itself, was not unusual, but the fright with which the natives heard the news was. The chief was nothing to them; in fact he was something of a villain, but his killing seemed to inspire them with a fright that was little short of homicidal. When the black reaches a certain stage of fear, he is as dangerous as a cornered panther. The next time Senecoza called, they rose and fled en masse and did not return until he had taken his departure.

Between the fear of the blacks, the tearing to pieces of the chief by the hyenas, and the fetish-man, I seemed to sense vaguely a connection of some kind. But I could not grasp the intangible thought.

Not long thereafter, that thought was intensified by another incident. I had ridden far out on the veldt, accompanied by my servant. As we paused to rest our horses close to a kopje, I saw, upon the top, a hyena eyeing us. Rather surprised, for the beasts are not in the habit of thus boldly approaching man in the daytime, I raised my rifle and was taking a steady aim, for I always hated the things, when my servant caught my arm.

"No shoot, *bwana*! No shoot!" he exclaimed hastily, jabbering a great deal in his own language, with which I was not familiar.

"What's up?" I asked impatiently.

He kept on jabbering and pulling my arm, until I gathered that the hyena was a fetish-beast of some kind.

"Oh, all right," I conceded, lowering my rifle just as the hyena turned and sauntered out of sight.

Something about the lank, repulsive beast and his shambling yet gracefully lithe walk struck my sense of humor with a ludicrous comparison.

Laughing, I pointed toward the beast and said, "That fellow looks like a hyena-imitation of Senecoza, the fetish-man." My simple statement seemed to throw the native into a more abject fear than ever.

He turned his pony and dashed off in the general direction of the ranch, looking back at me with a scared face.

I followed, annoyed. And as I rode I pondered. Hyenas, a fetish-man, a chief torn to pieces, a countryside of natives in fear; what was the connection? I puzzled and puzzled, but I was new to Africa; I was young and impatient, and presently with a shrug of annoyance I discarded the whole problem.

The next time Senecoza came to the ranch, he managed to stop directly in front of me. For a fleeting instant his glittering eyes looked into mine. And in spite of myself, I shuddered and stepped back, involuntarily, feeling much as a man feels who looks unaware into the eyes of a serpent. There was nothing tangible, nothing on which I could base a quarrel, but there was a distinct threat. Before my Nordic pugnacity could reassert itself, he was gone. I said nothing. But I knew that Senecoza hated me for some reason and that he plotted my killing. Why, I did not know.

As for me, my distrust grew into bewildered rage, which in turn became hate.

And then Ellen Farel came to the ranch. Why she should choose a trading-ranch in East Africa for a place to rest from the society life of New York, I do not know. Africa is no place for a woman. That is what Ludtvik, also a cousin of hers, told her, but he was overjoyed to see her. As for me, girls never interested me much; usually I felt like a fool in their presence and was glad to be out. But there were few whites in the vicinity and I tired of the company of Ludtvik.

Ellen was standing on the wide veranda when I first saw her, a slim, pretty young thing, with rosy cheeks and hair like gold and large gray eyes. She was surprisingly winsome in her costume of riding-breeches, puttees, jacket and light helmet.

I felt extremely awkward, dusty and stupid as I sat on my wiry African pony and stared at her.

She saw a stocky youth of medium height, with sandy hair, eyes in which a kind of gray predominated; an ordinary, unhandsome youth, clad in dusty riding-clothes and a cartridge belt on one side of which was slung an ancient Colt of big caliber, and on the other a long, wicked hunting-knife.

I dismounted, and she came forward, hand outstretched.

"I'm Ellen," she said, "and I know you're Steve. Cousin Ludtvik has been telling me about you."

I shook hands, surprised at the thrill the mere touch of her hand gave me.

She was enthusiastic about the ranch. She was enthusiastic about everything. Seldom have I seen anyone who had more vigor and vim, more enjoyment of everything done. She fairly scintillated with mirth and gaiety.

Ludtvik gave her the best horse on the place, and we rode much about the ranch and over the veldt.

The blacks interested her much. They were afraid of her, not being used to white women. She would have been off her horse and playing with the pickaninnies if I had let her. She couldn't understand why she should treat the black people as dust beneath her feet. We had long arguments about it. I could not convince her, so I told her bluntly that she didn't know anything about it and she must do as I told her.

She pouted her pretty lips and called me a tyrant, and then was off over the veldt like an antelope, laughing at me over her shoulder, her hair blowing free in the breeze.

Tyrant! I was her slave from the first. Somehow the idea of becoming a lover never enter my mind. It was not the fact that she was several years older than I, or that she had a sweetheart (several of them, I think) back in New York. Simply, I worshipped her; her presence intoxicated me, and I could think of no more enjoyable existence than serving her as a devoted slave.

I was mending a saddle one day when she came running in.

"Oh, Steve!" she called; "there's the most romantic-looking savage! Come quick and tell me what his name is."

She led me out of the veranda.

"There he is," she said, naively pointing. Arms folded, haughty head thrown back, stood Senecoza.

Ludtvik who was talking to him, paid no attention to the girl until he had completed his business with the fetish-man; and then, turning, he took her arm and they went into the house together.

Again I was face to face with the savage; but this time he was not looking at me. With a rage amounting almost to madness, I saw that he was gazing after the girl. There was an expression in his serpentlike eyes--

On the instant my gun was out and leveled. My hand shook like a leaf with the intensity of my fury. Surely I must shoot Senecoza down like the snake he was, shoot him down and riddle him, shoot him into a shredded heap!

The fleeting expression left his eyes and they were fixed on me. Detached they seemed, inhuman in their sardonic calm. And I could not pull the trigger.

For a moment we stood, and then he turned and strode away, a magnificent figure, while I glared after him and snarled with helpless fury.

I sat down on the veranda. What a man of mystery was that savage! What strange power did he possess? Was I right, I wondered, in interpreting the fleeting expression as he gazed after the girl? It seemed to me, in my youth and folly, incredible that a black man, no matter what his rank, should look at a white woman as he did. Most astonishing of all, why could I not shoot him down?

I started as a hand touched my arm.

"What are thinking about, Steve?" asked Ellen, laughing. Then before I could say anything, "Wasn't that chief, or whatever he was, a fine specimen of a savage? He invited us to come to his kraal; is that what you call it? It's away off in the veldt somewhere, and we're going."

"No!" I exclaimed violently, springing up.

"Why Steve," she gasped recoiling, "how rude! He's a perfect gentleman, isn't he, Cousin Ludtvik?"

"*Ja*," nodded Ludtvik, placidly, "we go to his kraal sometime soon, maybe. A strong chief, that savage. His chief has perhaps good trade."

"No!" I repeated furiously. "*I'll* go if somebody has to! Ellen's not going near that beast!"

"Well, that's nice!" remarked Ellen, somewhat indignantly. "I guess you're my boss, mister man?"

With all her sweetness, she had a mind of her own. In spite of all I could do, they arranged to go to the fetish-man's village the next day.

That night the girl came out to me, where I sat on the veranda in the moonlight, and she sat down on the arm of my chair.

"You're not angry at me, are you, Steve?" she said, wistfully, putting her arm around my shoulders. "Not mad, are you?"

Mad? Yes, maddened by the touch of her soft body--such mad devotion as a slave feels. I wanted to grovel in the dust at her feet and kiss her dainty shoes. Will women never learn the effect they have on men?

I took her hand hesitantly and pressed it to my lips. I think she must have sensed some of my devotion.

"Dear Steve," she murmured, and the words were like a caress, "come, let's walk in the moonlight."

We walked outside the stockade. I should have known better, for I had no weapon but the big Turkish dagger I carried and used for a hunting-knife, but she wished to.

"Tell me about this Senecoza," she asked, and I welcomed the opportunity. And then I thought: what could I tell her? That hyenas had eaten a small chief of the Masai? That the natives feared the fetish-man? That he had looked at her?

And then the girl screamed as out of the tall grass leaped a vague shape, half-seen in the moonlight.

I felt a heavy, hairy form crash against my shoulders; keen fangs ripped my upflung arm. I went to the earth, fighting with frenzied horror. My jacket was slit to ribbons and the fangs were at my throat before I found and drew my knife and stabbed, blindly and savagely. I felt my blade rip

13

into my foe, and then, like a shadow, it was gone. I staggered to my feet, somewhat shaken. The girl caught and steadied me.

"What was it?" she gasped, leading me toward the stockade.

"A hyena," I answered. "I could tell by the scent. But I never heard of one attacking like that."

She shuddered. Later on, after my torn arm had been bandaged, she came close to me and said in a wondrously subdued voice, "Steve, I've decided not to go to the village, if you don't want me to."

After the wounds on my arm had become scars Ellen and I resumed our rides, as might be expected. One day we had wandered rather far out on the veldt, and she challenged me to a race. Her horse easily distanced mine, and she stopped and waited for me, laughing.

She had stopped on a sort of kopje, and she pointed to a clump of trees some distance away.

"Trees!" she said gleefully. "Let's ride down there. There are so few trees on the veldt."

And she dashed away. I followed some instinctive caution, loosening my pistol in its holster, and, drawing my knife, I thrust it down in my boot so that it was entirely concealed.

We were perhaps halfway to the trees when from the tall grass about us leaped Senecoza and some twenty warriors.

One seized the girl's bridle and the others rushed me. The one who caught at Ellen went down with a bullet between his eyes, and another crumpled at my second shot. Then a thrown war-club hurled me from the saddle, half-senseless, and as the blacks closed in on me I saw Ellen's horse, driven frantic by the prick of a carelessly handled spear, scream and rear, scattering the blacks who held her, and dash away at headlong speed, the bit in her teeth.

I saw Senecoza leap on my horse and give chase, flinging a savage command over his shoulder; and both vanished over the kopje.

The warriors bound me hand and foot and carried me into the trees. A hut stood among them--a native hut of thatch and bark. Somehow the sight of it set me shuddering. It seemed to lurk, repellent and indescribably malevolent amongst the trees; to hint of horrid and obscene rites; of voodoo.

I know not why it is, but the sight of a native hut, alone and hidden, far from a village or tribe, always has to me a suggestion of nameless horror. Perhaps that is because only a black who is crazed or one who is so criminal that he has been exiled by his tribe will dwell that way.

In front of the hut they threw me down.

"When Senecoza returns with the girl," said they, "you will enter." And they laughed like fiends. Then, leaving one black to see that I did not escape, they left.

The black who remained kicked me viciously; he was a bestial-looking Negro, armed with a trade-musket.

"They go to kill white men, fool!" he mocked me. "They go to the ranches and trading-posts, first to that fool of an Englishman." Meaning Smith, the owner of a neighboring ranch.

And he went on giving details. Senecoza had made the plot, he boasted. They would chase all the white men to the coast.

"Senecoza is more than a man," he boasted. "You shall see, white man," lowering his voice and glancing about him, from beneath his low, beetling brows; "you shall see the magic of Senecoza." And he grinned, disclosing teeth filed to points.

"Cannibal!" I ejaculated, involuntarily. "A Masai?"

"No," he answered. "A man of Senecoza."

"Who will kill no white men," I jeered.

He scowled savagely. "I will kill you, white man."

"You dare not."

"That is true," he admitted, and added angrily, "Senecoza will kill you himself."

And meantime Ellen was riding like mad, gaining on the fetish-man, but unable to ride toward the ranch, for he had gotten between and was forcing her steadily out upon the veldt.

The black unfastened my bonds. His line of reasoning was easy to see; absurdly easy. He could not kill a prisoner of the fetish-man, but he could kill him to prevent his escape. And he was maddened with the blood-lust. Stepping back, he half-raised his trade-musket, watching me as a snake watches a rabbit.

It must have been about that time, as she afterward told me, that Ellen's horse stumbled and threw her. Before she could rise, the black had leaped from his horse and seized her in his arms. She screamed and fought, but he gripped her, held her helpless and laughed at her. Tearing her jacket to pieces, he bound her arms and legs, remounted and started back, carrying the half-fainting girl in front of him.

Back in front of the hut I rose slowly. I rubbed my arms where the ropes had been, moved a little closer to the black, stretched, stooped and rubbed my legs; then with a catlike bound I was on him, my knife flashing from my boot. The trade-musket crashed and the charge whizzed above my head as I knocked up the barrel and closed with him. Hand to hand, I would have been no match for the black giant; but I had the knife. Clinched close together we were too close for him to use the trade-musket for a club. He wasted time trying to do that, and with a desperate effort I threw him off his balance and drove the dagger to the hilt in his black chest.

I wrenched it out again; I had no other weapon, for I could find no more ammunition for the trade-musket.

I had no idea which way Ellen had fled. I assumed she had gone toward the ranch, and in that direction I took my way. Smith must be warned. The warriors were far ahead of me. Even then they might be creeping up about the unsuspecting ranch.

I had not covered a fourth of the distance, when a drumming of hoofs behind me caused me to turn my head. Ellen's horse was thundering toward me, riderless. I caught her as she raced past me, and managed to stop her. The story was plain. The girl had either reached a place of safety and had turned the horse loose, or what was much more likely, had been captured, the horse escaping and fleeing toward the ranch, as a horse will do. I gripped the saddle, torn with indecision. Finally I leaped on the horse and sent her flying toward Smith's ranch. It was not many miles; Smith must not be massacred by those black devils, and I must find a gun if I escaped to rescue the girl from Senecoza.

A half-mile from Smith's I overtook the raiders and went through them like drifting smoke. The workers at Smith's place were startled by a wild-riding horseman charging headlong into the stockade, shouting, "Masai! Masai! A raid, you fools!" snatching a gun and flying out again.

So when the savages arrived they found everybody ready for them, and they got such a warm reception that after one attempt they turned tail and fled back across the veldt.

And I was riding as I never rode before. The mare was almost exhausted, but I pushed her mercilessly. On, on!

I aimed for the only place I knew likely. The hut among the trees. I assumed that the fetish-man would return there.

And long before the hut came into sight, a horseman dashed from the grass, going at right angles to my course, and our horses, colliding, sent both tired animals to the ground.

"Steve!" It was a cry of joy mingled with fear. Ellen lay, tied hand and foot, gazing up at me wildly as I regained my feet.

Senecoza came with a rush, his long knife flashing in the sunlight. Back and forth we fought--slash, ward and parry, my ferocity and agility matching his savagery and skill.

A terrific lunge which he aimed at me, I caught on my point, laying his arm open, and then with a quick engage and wrench, disarmed him. But before I could use my advantage, he sprang away into the grass and vanished.

I caught up the girl, slashing her bonds, and she clung to me, poor child, until I lifted her and carried her toward the horses. But we were not yet through with Senecoza. He must have had a rifle cached away somewhere in the bush, for the first I knew of him was when a bullet spat within a foot above my head.

I caught at the bridles, and then I saw that the mare had done all she could, temporarily. She was exhausted. I swung Ellen up on the horse.

"Ride for our ranch," I ordered her. "The raiders are out, but you can get through. Ride low and ride fast!"

"But you, Steve!"

"Go, go!" I ordered, swinging her horse around and starting it. She dashed away, looking at me wistfully over her shoulder. Then I snatched the rifle and a handful of cartridges I had gotten at Smith's, and took to the bush. And through the hot African day, Senecoza and I played a game of hide-and-seek. Crawling, slipping in and out of the scanty veldt-bushes, crouching in the tall grass, we traded shots back and forth. A movement of the grass, a snapping twig, the rasp of grass-blades, and a bullet came questing, another answering it.

I had but a few cartridges and I fired carefully, but presently I pushed my one remaining cartridge into the rifle--a big, six-bore, single-barrel breech-loader, for I had not had time to pick when I snatched it up.

I crouched in my covert and watched for the black to betray himself by a careless movement. Not a sound, not a whisper among the grasses. Away off over the veldt a hyena sounded his fiendish laugh and another answered, closer at hand. The cold sweat broke out on my brow.

What was that? A drumming of many horses' hoofs! Raiders returning? I ventured a look and could have shouted for joy. At least twenty men were sweeping toward me, white men and ranch-boys, and ahead of them all rode Ellen! They were still some distance away. I darted behind a tall bush and rose, waving my hand to attract their attention.

They shouted and pointed to something beyond me. I whirled and saw, some thirty yards away, a huge hyena slinking toward me, rapidly. I glanced carefully across the veldt. Somewhere out there, hidden by the billowing grasses, lurked Senecoza. A shot would betray to him my position--and I had but one cartridge. The rescue party was still out of range.

I looked again at the hyena. He was still rushing toward me. There was no doubt as to his intentions. His eyes glittered like a fiend's from Hell, and a scar on his shoulder showed him to be the same beast that had once before attacked me. Then a kind of horror took hold of me, and resting the old elephant rifle over my elbow, I sent my last bullet crashing through the bestial thing. With a scream that seemed to have a horribly human note in it, the hyena turned and fled back into the bush, reeling as it ran.

And the rescue party swept up around me.

A fusillade of bullets crashed through the bush from which Senecoza had sent his last shot. There was no reply.

"Ve hunt ter snake down," quoth Cousin Ludtvik, his Boer accent increasing with his excitement. And we scattered through the veldt in a skirmish line, combing every inch of it warily.

Not a trace of the fetish-man did we find. A rifle we found, empty, with empty shells scattered about, and (which was very strange) *hyena tracks leading away from the rifle.*

I felt the short hairs of my neck bristle with intangible horror. We looked at each other, and said not a word, as with a tacit agreement we took up the trail of the hyena.

We followed it as it wound in and out in the shoulder-high grass, showing how it had slipped up on me, stalking me as a tiger stalks its victim. We struck the trail the thing had made, returning to the bush after I had shot it. Splashes of blood marked the way it had taken. We followed.

"It leads toward the fetish-hut," muttered an Englishman. "Here, sirs, is a damnable mystery."

And Cousin Ludtvik ordered Ellen to stay back, leaving two men with her.

We followed the trail over the kopje and into the clump of trees. Straight to the door of the hut it led. We circled the hut cautiously, but no tracks led away. It was inside the hut. Rifles ready, we forced the rude door.

No tracks led away from the hut and no tracks led to it except the tracks of the hyena. Yet there was no hyena within that hut; and on the dirt floor, a bullet through his black breast, lay Senecoza, the fetish-man.

THE END